Three Little Pigs

Key sound igh spellings: i, igh, y
Secondary sounds: aw, short oo, ck

Written by Nick Page
Illustrated by Clare Fennell

Reading with phonics

How to use this book

The **Reading with phonics** series helps you to have fun with your child and to support their learning of phonics and reading. It is aimed at children who have learned the letter sounds and are building confidence in their reading.

Each title in the series focuses on a different key sound. The entertaining retelling of the story repeats this sound frequently, and the different spellings for the sound are highlighted in red type. The first activity at the back of the book provides practice in reading and using words that contain this sound. The key sound for **Three Little Pigs** is igh.

Start by reading the story to your child, asking them to join in with the refrain in bold. Next, encourage them to read the story with you. Give them a hand to decode tricky words.

Now look at the activity pages at the back of the book. These are intended for you and your child to enjoy together. Most are not activities to complete in pencil or pen, but by reading and talking or pointing.

The **Key sound** pages focus on one sound, and on the various different groups of letters that produce that sound. Encourage your child to read the different letter groups and complete the activity, so they become more aware of the variety of spellings there are for the same sound.

The **Letters together** pages look at three pairs or groups of letters and at the sounds they make as they work together. Help your child to read the words and trace the route on the word maps.

Rhyme is used a lot in these retellings. Whatever stage your child has reached in their learning of phonics, it is always good practice for them to listen carefully for sounds and spot words that rhyme. The pages on **Rhyming words** take six words from the story and ask children to read and spot other words that rhyme with them.

The **Key words** pages focus on a number of key words that occur regularly but can nonetheless be tricky. Many of these words are not sounded out following the rules of phonics and the easiest thing is for children to learn them by sight, so that they do not worry about decoding them. These pages encourage children to retell the story, practising key words as they do so.

The **Picture dictionary** page asks children to focus closely on nine words from the story. Encourage children to look carefully at each word, cover it with their hand, write it on a separate piece of paper, and finally, check it!

Do not complete all the activities at once – doing one each time you read will ensure that your child continues to enjoy the stories and the time you are spending together. **Have fun!**

Bye, bye!

4

Three little pigs left home one day,
packed their bags and went on their way.
Mother Pig said, "Good-bye, bye, bye,"
while a wolf saw them go,
thinking, "My, my, my . . ."

My, my, my!

"I spy, with my little eye,
sausages, bacon, and pork pie!"

5

Little pig one spied a man selling straw.
"Try dry grass!" said the sign at the store.
The bales were light, and he stacked them high,
while the wolf licked his lips,
thinking, "My, my, my . . .

**I spy, with my little eye,
sausages, bacon, and pork pie!"**

Try dry grass!

Little pig two met a man selling wood.
"Right," she said, "this will look quite good."
The pile of wood was as high as the sky,
while the wolf licked his lips,
thinking, "My, my, my . . .

I spy, with my little eye,
sausages, bacon, and pork pie!"

My, my, my!

9

Little pig three met a man selling bricks.
They were mighty strong – much better
than sticks.
He built his house in the blink of an eye,
while the wolf licked his lips, thinking,
"My, my, my . . .

I spy, with my little eye,
sausages, bacon, and pork pie!"

Bricks

The homes were built that very same night,
and in went the pigs, to their delight.
Quite soon, the big, bad wolf came by,
licking his lips, thinking, "My, my, my . . ."

"I spy, with my little eye,
sausages, bacon, and pork pie!"

My, my, my!

Cried the wolf to Piggy Straw,
"Now let me in!"
"Not by the hair on my chinny chin chin!"
The wolf huffed and puffed
and the house went "WHAM"!
And the wolf licked his lips, shouting,
"Mmm, FRIED HAM!

I spy, with my little eye,
sausages, bacon, and pork pie!"

Huff!

Piggy Straw ran in fright to
the house of Piggy Wood.
Right behind was the wolf,
who was up to no good.
Then he huffed and he puffed
and the house went "SMASH"!
And the wolf licked his lips, shouting,
"Mmm, GOULASH!"

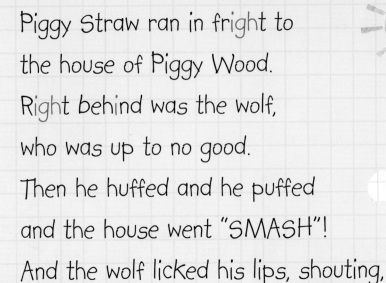

SMASH!

"I spy, with my little eye,
sausages, bacon, and pork pie!"

The pigs took flight to the house made of brick.
They were chased by the wolf
(who was not quite as quick).
There, he huffed and he puffed,
but the house stayed whole,
so the wolf climbed the roof,
shouting, "Mmm, CASSEROLE!

I spy, with my little eye,
sausages, bacon, and pork pie!"

The pigs heard the wolf climb
higher and higher.
"Quick, get a pot and light the fire!"
The wolf jumped right down the
chimney tower,
landed in the pot, and cried,
"OW! SWEET AND SOUR!

I spy, with my little eye,
sausages, bacon, and pork pie!"

Ow!

The wolf jumped up
and ran outside.
He cried out loud:
"My poor backside!"

22

As the wolf ran away at the speed of light,
the three little pigs sang with delight,

Ow!

"I spy, with my little eye,
a big, bad wolf saying bye, bye, bye."

Key sound

There are several different groups of letters that make the **igh** sound. Practise them by playing a game of "I spy" with the wolf! Choose a cloud and put as many of its words as you can in an "I spy" sentence. For example: I spy with my little eye a **bright knight** in a **mighty fright**!

knight

high

light

sight

sigh

bright

night

mighty

right

fright

tights

crisis   child

pirate

wild   idea

silent   pilot

dry

by   my   why

supply   cry

try   fry

fly   shy

mice

rice   hide   kite

file   time   bike

wife   fine

while   bite

25

Letters together

Look at these pairs of letters and say the sounds they make.

aw　**oo**　**ck**

Follow the words that contain **aw** to help the first little pig buy straw for his house.

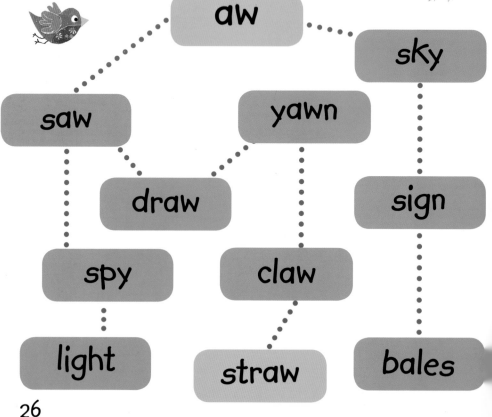

aw

sky

saw

yawn

draw

sign

spy

claw

light

straw

bales

Follow the words that contain the **short oo** to help this little pig buy some wood.

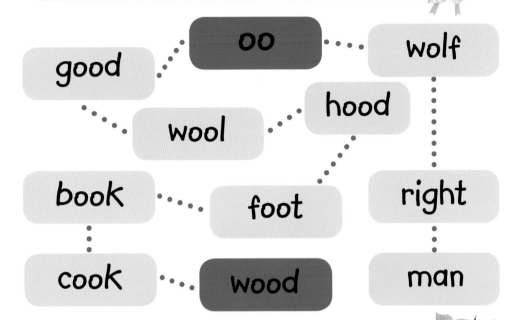

good

oo

wolf

wool

hood

book

foot

right

cook

wood

man

Follow the words that contain **ck** to help this little pig buy bricks for his house.

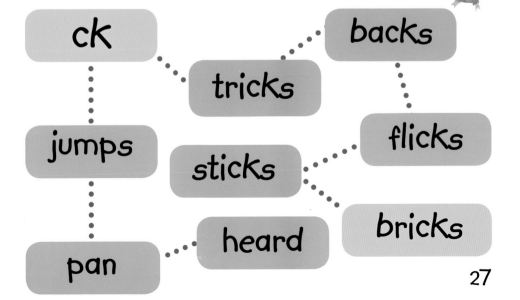

ck

backs

tricks

jumps

flicks

sticks

bricks

heard

pan

27

Rhyming words

Read the words in the flowers and point to other words that rhyme with them.

twig	**pig**	wood
wig		wolf

house	**straw**	pie
claw		saw

chicks	**sticks**	store
ran		bricks

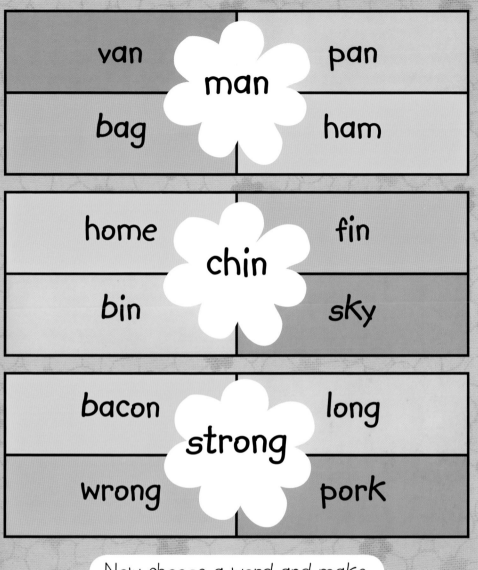

van	pan
bag	ham

man

home	fin
bin	sky

chin

bacon	long
wrong	pork

strong

Now choose a word and make up a rhyming chant!

I cry "bye" as I spy a fried pie.

Key words

Many common words can be tricky to sound out. Practise them by reading these sentences about the story. Now make more sentences using other Key words from around the border.

The wolf **asked** the pigs to let him in.

One pig **found** a man selling wood.

The pigs **would** not open the door.

man • took

• can't • didn't • asked • he • food • been • stop • would

Three little pigs left home **one** day.

The wolf wanted the pigs for **food**.

The wolf **could** not blow down the brick house.

One pig bought **lots** of bricks.

The wolf huffed and **he** puffed.

One pig chose to **live** in a house made of straw.

The wolf **went** down the chimney and landed in hot water.

went • lots • need • that's • gave • may • still • found • live • soon • night • one • say

made • way • could • these • began • next • first •

Picture dictionary

Look carefully at the pictures and the words.
Now cover the words, one at a time.
Can you remember how to write them?

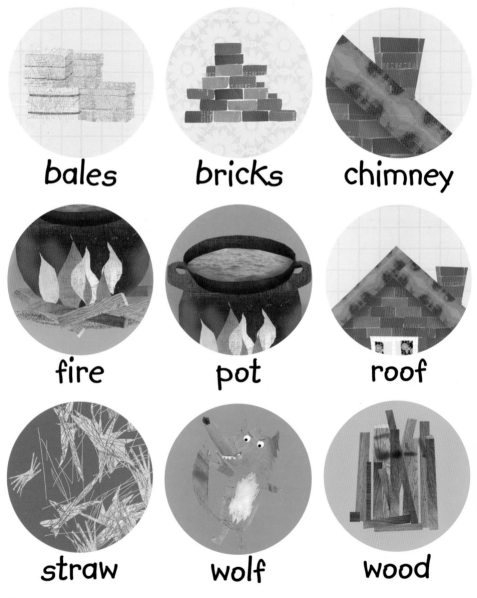

bales   **bricks**   **chimney**

fire   **pot**   **roof**

straw   **wolf**   **wood**